D0246966

TWO FROGS

Chris Wormell

TED SMART

ONCE THERE WERE TWO FROGS sitting on a lily pad
in the middle of a large pond.

One of the frogs was holding a stick.
"What's that for?" asked the other frog.

"For protection," said the frog with the stick.

"This stick is to beat off the dog."

"What dog?" said the other frog, quickly looking over his shoulder. "I can't see a dog. There is no dog!"

"Not now there isn't, not at this moment," replied the frog with the stick. "But what if a dog should come swimming across the pond and try to eat us up? Better safe than sorry."

The other frog was puzzled. "But no dogs ever come swimming in this pond," he protested. "At least I've never seen one. In fact I can't even remember seeing one on the edge of the pond. And why would a dog want to come swimming in the pond anyway? They're not so fond of swimming as us frogs, you know."

"Perhaps the dog's master might throw a ball out into the pond for him to fetch," suggested the frog with the stick.

"But this is such a large pond it would have to be a mighty throw to reach us out here," declared the other frog.

"And the dog would have to be a very good swimmer!"

"But suppose the dog's master was a champion javelin thrower?" suggested the frog with the stick. "Suppose a champion javelin thrower came to this pond with his dog (who was an excellent swimmer) and threw the ball right out here to the middle for his dog to fetch. And what if the dog, while fetching the ball, came upon us frogs and tried to eat us up? Well, I have a stick to beat off the dog!"

The other frog burst out laughing. "Foolish frog!" he cried. "You're much more likely to be eaten by a pike or a heron than by a dog. Why worry about dogs? It's ridiculous!"

He laughed so much he fell into the pond.

Just at that moment, a large pike was swimming by
beneath the lily pads.

It heard the plop of the frog falling in...

It opened its enormous toothy jaws and was just

about to gobble up the two frogs...

when a heron snapped them up in its beak.

It flew off, leaving the large pike chewing on a lily pad.

But...

the stick jammed in the heron's beak as it tried to swallow
the two frogs.

They jumped out and fell back into the pond – plop! plop!

As soon as they hit the water the two frogs swam as fast as they could to the shore and hopped off into the woods looking for sticks.

So they missed the champion javelin thrower who came

to the pond that morning with his dog...

For Jack and Mary

TWO FROGS

This edition produced for The Book People Ltd,
Hall Wood Avenue, Haydock, St Helens, WA11 9UL

First published in Great Britain by Jonathan Cape,
an imprint of Random House Children's Books

Jonathan Cape edition published 2003
The Book People edition published 2003

1 3 5 7 9 10 8 6 4 2

Copyright © Chris Wormell, 2003

The right of Chris Wormell
to be identified as the author and illustrator of this work
has been asserted in accordance with the Copyright, Designs and Patents Act 1988.

All rights reserved. No part of this publication may be reproduced,
stored in a retrieval system, or transmitted in any form or by any means,
electronic, mechanical, photocopying, recording or otherwise,
without the prior permission of the publishers.

RANDOM HOUSE CHILDREN'S BOOKS
61–63 Uxbridge Road, London W5 5SA
A division of The Random House Group Ltd

RANDOM HOUSE AUSTRALIA (PTY) LTD
20 Alfred Street, Milsons Point, Sydney,
New South Wales 2061, Australia

RANDOM HOUSE NEW ZEALAND LTD
18 Poland Road, Glenfield, Auckland 10, New Zealand

RANDOM HOUSE (PTY) LTD
Endulini, 5A Jubilee Road, Parktown 2193, South Africa

THE RANDOM HOUSE GROUP Limited Reg. No. 954009

A CIP catalogue record for this book is available from the British Library.

Printed in Hong Kong